LUCKY BUNNIES

Ruby's Red Skates

Hop into every adventure!

LUCKY BUNNIES:
Ruby's Red Skates

by Catherine Coe

Scholastic Inc.

For Mum, for everything xxx

Copyright © 2020 by Catherine Coe

ISBN 978-1-3386-1101-4

10 9 8 7 6 5 4 3 2 1   20 21 22 23 24

Printed in the U.S.A.   40
First printing 2020
Book design by Stephanie Yang

Contents

n
LUCK RAINBOW
CLOVER TRAIN
WARREN STREET
SPARKLE RIVER
PINEAPPLE
SQUARE
DANDELION
SCHOOL

Bright Burrow

BASIL FOREST

MIRROR LAKE

PARADISE BEACH

RADISH HIGH SCHOOL

CUCUMBER ROW

HAY ARENA

CARROT CENTRAL

STRAWBERRY FIELDS

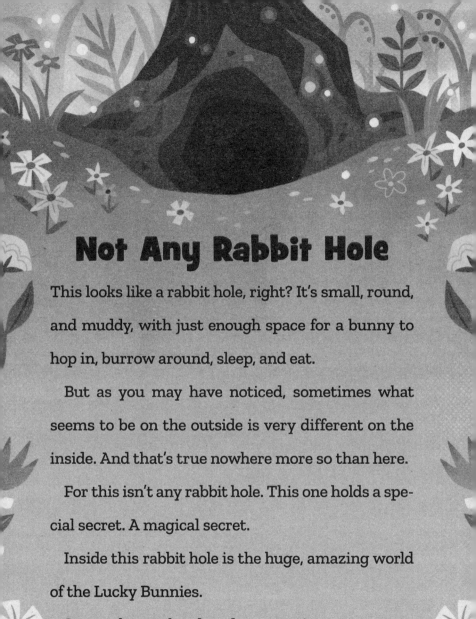

Not Any Rabbit Hole

This looks like a rabbit hole, right? It's small, round, and muddy, with just enough space for a bunny to hop in, burrow around, sleep, and eat.

But as you may have noticed, sometimes what seems to be on the outside is very different on the inside. And that's true nowhere more so than here.

For this isn't any rabbit hole. This one holds a special secret. A magical secret.

Inside this rabbit hole is the huge, amazing world of the Lucky Bunnies.

So watch your head, and come on in.

Welcome to the magical land of Bright Burrow . . .

ONE
Wishing for Snow

Ruby breathed in deeply as she cleaned her brand-new, shiny red ice skates with a fern cloth. She loved the smell of new shoes, and these were extra special—she'd wanted them for ages before her parents bought them for her birthday. All Ruby needed now was for it to get cold and icy enough

for Mirror Lake to ice over so she could use them!

It had been warm and sunny recently, but with the Weather Rabbit, that could change in an instant. The Weather Rabbit was a mechanical creature who lived in the clock tower in Pineapple Square. He was in charge of the weather, and so far he'd never listened to Ruby nor any of her friends when they'd asked him to change it. Ruby knew it wouldn't be worth trying, even though she wanted it to snow SO badly!

With a sigh, she laid the red ice skates back in their box, fastened the lid, and put the box back in the cupboard. Beside it sat her fluffy earmuffs and matching scarf. She tugged the

earmuffs over her long red ears and wrapped the scarf around her neck. Ruby looked in the mirror beside the cupboard and beamed. She loved the winter and all the warm, fluffy clothes that went with it.

Ruby wouldn't just go ice-skating, she'd also make snow bunnies . . . and go sledding and . . .

Before she forgot anything, Ruby ran to her bedroom and started a new list in her notebook:

My list of must-do winter things,

- *Ice-skating on Mirror Lake*
- *Building snow bunnies*
- *Sledding down Strawberry Fields*
- *Having a snowball fight*
- *Making snow burrows*

Ruby twiddled her barkpen around in her paw as she thought hard in case she'd missed something. She stopped when she heard a knock at the burrow door. Her parents and sister were out shopping on Cucumber Row, so Ruby rushed to answer it.

She pulled it open and smiled. A very fluffy blue bunny was standing on the doorstep.

"Hi, Sky!" Ruby said, and beckoned her friend inside.

But Sky stood on the spot, staring at the top of Ruby's head. "Hey, are you okay, Ruby?" Sky

asked in her chirpy voice. "Do you have a cold or something?"

Ruby frowned for a moment, wondering what Sky was talking about, until she remembered that she was still wearing her earmuffs. "Oh no, I'm totally fine!" She whipped off the earmuffs and grinned. "I was just trying them on."

Sky looked behind her, still feeling confused. Bright Burrow was filled with warm sunshine and there wasn't a cloud in the sky. "I don't think you'll need those today!"

"I know," Ruby replied. "But I just can't wait for it to snow and to use my new ice skates. Do you want to see them?"

Sky did a backflip. "Sure thing! Are these

the ones your parents got you for your birthday?"

Ruby nodded as she led Sky to the cupboard and took the box out carefully.

"What's an ice skate's favorite greeting?" Sky asked with a grin.

Ruby twitched her whiskers, trying to think of an answer to Sky's joke. "Good skating?" she guessed, although it didn't sound very funny.

"No," said Sky. "Have an ice day!"

Ruby giggled at Sky's joke as she lifted the ice skates out of the box. Sky oohed and aahed at the beautiful red skates. "They're amazing!" she said, stroking one with her fluffy blue paw. "No wonder you can't wait to skate in them. I'm sure the Weather

Rabbit will make it snow soon."

"I hope so!" Ruby said, thinking about the list she'd made of all the fun things she and her friends could do.

"Are you ready to leave for the game?" Sky asked. She, Ruby, and their four best friends were going to Hay Arena to watch a bunny

basketball game. They were even more excited than usual because Petal's mom was playing!

"Let me just put the skates away." Ruby laid them back in the box and shut the cupboard. Then she scribbled a quick note for her parents on a piece of bark paper so they would know where she was when they got home. "All right, I'm ready!"

Sky spun on her toes, suddenly just a blur of blue fur. "Let's go!" she said, jumping up and punching the air.

TWO
Bunny Basketball

Sky, Ruby, Petal, Star, Twinkle, and Diamond sat on one of the hay bales stacked at the front of Hay Arena. Petal's mom had reserved it for them so they could see her playing up close. Twinkle swung his legs back and forth as he perched on the hay bale, clapping his mint-green paws.

"This is going to be furbulous!" he said.

The rest of the friends began clapping as the bunny basketball players ran onto the court, and Petal whooped with delight when she saw her mom. Petal's mom was even taller than Petal, with the same pink fur and extremely long, droopy ears—but she'd tied them back into a bow for the game.

"Go, Lucky Whiskers!" Petal shouted to the team, and her mom smiled and waved at Petal and her five best friends.

Soon the bunny referee blew her whistle and the game began.

"I want to be a basketball bunny when I grow up," Star said as they watched the other team, the Longtails, hit the side of the

hoop. "I can definitely bounce high enough!"

Her friends nodded as the Lucky Whiskers began attacking at the other end of the court. Star was chosen for the Bounce-a-Lot event every year, and practiced jumping every day, without fail.

One of the Lucky Whiskers' players passed the ball to Petal's mom, who leaped toward

the hoop ... for a slam dunk.

The bunny friends jumped up and cheered. "Well done, Mom!" Petal yelled, hoping her mom would hear her.

"Two to nothing, Lucky Whiskers!" Star

said, and nudged Petal as they sat back down and the game continued. "Do you think you'll become a basketball bunny?" Star asked Petal. "You know—follow in your mom's pawsteps?"

Petal shook her head so hard that one of her floppy ears swiped Star on the shoulder. "Oops-a-daisy. Sorry, Star. I didn't mean to hit you! No, I don't want to be a basketball bunny. I always trip over the ball when we play at school!"

A Lucky Whiskers player snatched the ball from one of the Longtails, and Petal's mom bounded into the corner. Petal held her breath as her mom lifted the ball for a shot . . . and it sailed straight in!

Petal squealed. "Woo-hoo! Incredible shot, Mom!"

The bunnies leaped up and down, hugging each other and shouting, "Go, Lucky Whiskers!"

"Go, Petal's mom!" Twinkle squeaked. "That shot was burrow-tastic!"

"It was the best basketball shot I've ever seen," said Diamond beside him, putting her white paws to her face in awe. "Petal's mom is a great player."

By the end of the first quarter, the Lucky Whiskers were winning 9–4. The bunny friends munched on handfuls of hay from the bales they were sitting on as they waited for the second quarter to begin.

"This is an amazing game," said Sky. "Actually, an amaze*balls* game! I *hoop* the Lucky Whiskers win."

Star groaned and Sky shrugged. "You like my jokes really, Star," Sky told her. "I know you do!"

The second quarter began, and soon the Lucky Whiskers were up 15–6. But then Diamond noticed something. "Is your mom limping?" she asked Petal.

Petal gasped. Her mom was still running, but she could tell something was wrong by the way her mom kept wincing. She went to intercept a Longtails player but instead of getting the ball, she collapsed to the floor. "Mom!" Petal yelped as her mom was

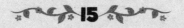

helped off the court and replaced by another player. Her mom shook her head as one of the coaches put ice on the hurt ankle.

I hope she isn't too badly hurt! Petal thought.

Just a minute later, the game stopped for halftime. "I'm going to check on my mom," Petal told her friends, her face clouded with worry. She raced toward the changing rooms, almost tripping on an ear as she went.

"Petal should tie her ears up like her mom does," Ruby said. "She'd trip over them much less then!"

Diamond nodded. "I hope her mom's okay," she said.

"The Lucky Whiskers have the *best* coaches,"

Star replied. "They'll be taking care of Petal's mom. It looked like just a sprain to me."

"But it super-stinks that she won't be able to play in the second half." Twinkle twitched his little green nose.

"Maybe she'll recover quickly and get back in the game!" said Sky, always the most optimistic of the friends.

But when the Lucky Whiskers team came back out to start the second half, Petal's mom wasn't with them.

"At least Petal is with her," Ruby said. "I'm sure that'll make her mom feel a lot better."

The five bunnies watched the third and fourth quarters, oohing, aahing, and cheering

every time the Lucky Whiskers team scored.
As the referee blew her whistle for the end of
the game, Ruby looked over at the scoreboard.
It was 25–14, a win for the Lucky Whiskers!
The friends leaped up and celebrated as the
basketball bunnies shook hands with each
other on the court.

"Lucky Whiskers! Lucky Whiskers!" their fans yelled as the team ran a lap around the court, waving their paws to all their supporters.

Eventually, the basketball bunnies left the court and everyone began filing out of Hay Arena.

"Should we wait for Petal?" Diamond wondered just as Petal popped up beside them.

"Mom's sprained her ankle," Petal explained. "I'm going to go home with her."

"Please congratulate her on winning the game," said Star.

"It was totally awesome!" Ruby added. "Apart from when your mom got hurt, of course."

"We hope she's back to burrow-strength soon," Twinkle squeaked. "What bad luck to get injured. She was the Lucky Whiskers' star player!"

"Thanks," said Petal. "I'll tell her that!" She turned and almost bumped into another bunny going the other way as she rushed off back toward the locker room.

The rest of the friends left Hay Arena and began scampering toward Warren Street, where they all lived.

As they neared Pineapple Square, Diamond spotted the Weather Rabbit popping out of the clock tower on a mechanical arm. "Look!" she said to her friends, and they all stopped and turned toward the silver bunny.

"Oh snow, oh snow, send us your snowflakes!" the Weather Rabbit called.

Ruby cartwheeled with excitement. "It's
going to snow!" she said as she turned
upright again. Sure enough, the sky had
filled with thick white clouds and the first
snowflakes were already drifting down. She

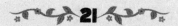

crossed her fingers on each of her paws. If it kept snowing, then Mirror Lake would ice over, and Ruby would finally be able to use her skates!

THREE
Time to Skate!

Luckily, it snowed for the next four days straight. After school, the six friends went to play in the snow every day. On Monday they built snow bunnies, on Tuesday they sledded down Strawberry Fields, on Wednesday they made snow burrows, and on Thursday they had a snowball fight.

But there was still one thing Ruby longed to do—the first thing on her list. Ice-skate on Mirror Lake! It was all the bunnies at Dandelion School could talk about, but they had to wait until the lake was properly iced over.

When Ruby woke up on Friday, the first thing she did was run to the front door to look out and see whether it was still snowing, just like she'd done every day this week. It was! She washed herself, gulped down her breakfast of mint and carrot porridge, and pulled on her scarf and earmuffs. The quicker she was, the more time she'd have for playing in the snow before school.

Outside her burrow, Ruby began rolling a snowball, pushing it in one line, then turning

around and rolling it back, a bit like her mom did when she mowed the lawn. Soon the ball was almost as big as she was! Next, she made another, smaller, ball—for the head—and then started to shape one bunny ear.

"Hey, Ruby!" called Sky from behind her. "Are you coming to school?"

Ruby looked up and saw lots of young bunnies leaving their burrows on Warren Street. She nodded at Sky and said, "Can you wait just a moment? I need to put my tie on!"

Sky smiled and Ruby ran inside, found her school tie and bag, and rushed out again. Now, it wasn't just Sky outside, but Diamond, Star, Twinkle, and Petal.

"What do snow bunnies do when they're upset?" asked Sky.

"What?" squeaked Twinkle as the others shrugged.

"Have a meltdown!" Sky kicked her feet in the air as she said the punch line, and everyone else giggled.

They began scampering toward Dandelion School. Everything around them was carpeted in a layer of white snow—even the clock tower in the distance.

Please don't change the weather, Ruby thought when she passed the clock tower, worrying the Weather Rabbit might pop out at any moment. But it kept on snowing, big flakes floating down all around them.

"I love the sound the snow makes under my paws!" said Petal, listening for the shuddering cracking sound each time she took another step.

Twinkle tried to listen for it, but he couldn't hear anything at all. *Maybe it's because my paws are much, much smaller than Petal's. Or maybe because she has furbulous hearing!* he thought.

"Will you be able to play in the snow after school today, Petal?" Twinkle asked. Petal had been helping out at home after her mom had been injured playing bunny basketball.

"I don't think so," Petal replied. "Mom's ankle's getting better, but she still can't really walk on it."

"I'm sorry you've been missing out," Diamond said, but Petal smiled.

"Don't worry about me. This isn't my favorite weather. I fall over even more than usual when it's snowy and icy. I'm quite happy being at home in the warmth!"

They reached their classroom at Dandelion School, inside the trunk of an oak tree. The friends stomped their paws outside so they didn't bring too much snow in, then ran to their desks.

For once, Mr. Nibble wasn't eating anything. Their teacher was almost always nibbling on a

carrot or some berries or a stick of celery. But today he was simply standing at the front of the classroom with a huge smile on his black-and-white face.

"Take your places, Oak Class," he said. "Come on, quickly now." He clapped his paws together and added, "I have some exciting news . . ."

Everyone took a breath and a few of the bunnies started whispering about what it might be.

Mr. Nibble clapped his hands again so they'd quiet down. "The news is . . . Mirror Lake is now ready to skate on!"

Ruby leaped up and punched the air. "Awesome!" She turned to Twinkle, grinning. "We can finally go skating!"

"Burrow-tastic!" Twinkle squeaked back.

Mr. Nibble wrote on the barkboard:

Staying safe when skating on Mirror Lake

1 . . .

Ooh, a list! thought Ruby. She watched carefully as Mr. Nibble started writing the list, and got out her barkbook to copy it.

1. *Always look where you're going, even when skating backward.*
2. *Look out for other skaters and don't get too close.*
3. *If you feel tired or cold, stop for a rest.*
4. *Make sure your skates fit properly to avoid injuries.*
5. *If you fall or get injured, move off the ice*

as quickly as possible. Ask an adult for

help if necessary.

Mr. Nibble turned around. "Skating on the lake is fun," he said. "But it's important to take care. This list of guidelines will help you stay safe. Please copy it down, everyone."

The class did as he said, chattering as they wrote. Mr. Nibble didn't seem to mind the noise and excitement. By the way he was beaming and hopping from paw to paw, he looked as excited as they did.

But they had to get through a whole day of lessons before they could go skating.

"Today is going so slowly," Star said when the bell rang for lunchtime.

"Totally!" Ruby agreed. After they'd eaten lunch, they had fun playing in the snow, and even made a game of bowling with some snow pins and a snowball. But all they could really think about was going to skate on Mirror Lake.

In the afternoon, they worked in groups on an art project, each making a collage about winter. It was the kind of thing that Twinkle loved, but even he couldn't sit still properly, because he was thinking about pulling on his skates and zooming about on the ice. It was almost like flying!

Diamond was starting to think the end-of-school bell would never come. *Perhaps the head teacher has forgotten to ring it*, she thought. *Maybe we'll be here all evening!*

But finally … *BRRRRING!* it rang and the entire class jumped out of their seats.

"Wait!" Mr. Nibble called. Everyone groaned. They just wanted to go home to pick up their skates and get on the ice! "I have a special announcement before you leave for the weekend." The class turned to face him.

What is it? thought Sky, bouncing from paw to paw. Going by the smile on Mr. Nibble's face, it had to be something good.

"Instead of lessons on Monday, we will be having a school trip to Mirror Lake. I've just arranged it! What's more, Poppy Lightpaw will be coming to give us all some ice-skating tips and tricks!"

Ruby couldn't help but let out a shriek. Poppy

Lightpaw was the winner of last year's Skate
to Be Great—an ice-skating tournament held
every year in Bright Burrow. Ruby had gone to
Hay Arena every day to watch it, even when
it'd been so cold she thought her nose might
fall off.

"We'll be meeting at Mirror Lake rather

than here first thing on Monday morning,"
Mr. Nibble went on. "And don't forget your ice
skates!"

Oak Class ran out of the tree trunk faster
than ever before. Diamond, Star, Twinkle,
Petal, Sky, and Ruby scampered home together,
all the while chattering about their school trip
on Monday.

"We're so lucky to have Poppy Lightpaw
coming to teach us!" said Ruby.

"And we have the whole weekend to skate
before then, too," Star added. "I'm going to
practice so hard. I want to show Poppy my
triple flip, and I have to make sure it's perfect!"

"Don't you mean *pawfect*?" Sky chuckled.

Ruby's heart fluttered like a butterfly at the

thought of using her new skates at last. She couldn't stop smiling. She had waited for this day for *such* a long time!

When they got to Warren Street, the bunnies ran off to their homes to pick up their skates. "Let's meet back at Mirror Lake?" Twinkle suggested before they went their separate ways. "That way we won't lose any skating time!"

Everyone but Petal nodded. "I'll probably need to help at home," she said. "But I'll absolutely try to come later. Have fun!"

Ruby hurried toward her burrow. "Hi, Mom!" she panted as she opened the door and rushed to the cupboard. She looked up to the shelf where she'd left her skates . . .

But the box wasn't there!

FOUR
The Skate Search

Ruby ran to her room. *Maybe I left them there instead?* she thought. But she was sure she'd put them back in the cupboard!

She sniffed deeply, making her curly whiskers tremble. With her excellent nose, she should be able to smell her ice skates if they were in here. And she couldn't detect a sniff

of the ice skates. Still, she started looking in
her wardrobe, in her drawers, and inside her
desk.

Perhaps the box is keeping the smell inside, she
said to herself, diving under her bed in case
she'd put it safely there.

By the time she'd finished, her room looked

like it had been tipped upside down. Ruby's clothes, toys, and school things were scattered all over—everything Ruby owned, except for her ice skates!

She wondered whether she should tidy the room, but she wanted to go and join her friends on Mirror Lake as soon as she could. They were sure to be ice-skating by now!

Ruby scampered out of her room and back to the cupboard. Perhaps they were on a different shelf, she decided, and started pulling everything out, sniffing and staring as she looked for the box.

"What are you doing, Ruby?" called her mom behind her.

"Um . . . looking for my scarf," Ruby fibbed.

She didn't like lying to her parents, but she knew they'd spent ages saving up to get her the new ice skates, and they'd be so disappointed if she'd lost them. "Here it is!" She pulled out the purple scarf and wrapped it around her neck, even though she was really warm from all the searching she'd been doing.

She put back the things from the cupboard hurriedly, knowing she would get into trouble if she left it a mess. She just hoped her mom didn't decide now was the moment to check and see if she'd been keeping her room tidy!

Ruby darted into the kitchen and began opening all the cupboards and drawers.

"Ruby, can you stop that?" her dad asked.

"I'm trying to prepare dinner and you're getting in my way. What are you looking for anyway?"

"Um ... um ... nothing!" Ruby said, rushing away before her dad could quiz her anymore.

She went back into her room, feeling her eyes fill with tears. She blinked them away. *Focus, Ruby,* she thought. *They'll be in the burrow somewhere!* Ruby cleared her desk and hopped onto the chair. She took out her notebook and chewed the end of her barkpen as she thought about where her skates might be. "They couldn't have disappeared!" she said to herself. She was determined to solve the problem somehow.

Ruby made a list of all the places in the burrow she'd already searched and a list of the places she hadn't, which were

- ~~Mom and Dad's bedroom~~
- *Squeak's bedroom*

She quickly crossed out Mom and Dad's bedroom because they wouldn't have taken her skates. But her sister, Squeak, might have! Ruby leaped up from her desk and ran into Squeak's room without knocking.

"Hey!" Squeak said. She was lying on the floor, playing with her bunnyhouse. "Didn't you see the sign?"

"What sign?" said Ruby.

"The one on the door that reads, 'KEEP OUT!'" Squeak replied.

Ruby sighed. "I just want to ask you a question."

Squeak sat up and sneezed. "*Achoo!*" She wiped her nose and said, "I'll answer your question if you promise to play with me."

"Not now, Squeak! Please, just tell me if you've seen my ice skates!"

"What ice skates?"

"The red ones—in the red box," Ruby said, trying not to get angry with her sister. "I'm sure I left them in the cupboard. Did you take them?"

Squeak shook her head. "Your new ones? *Achoo!* No, I haven't seen them. But Mom

and Dad won't be happy if you've lost them!"

"I know that!" Ruby huffed. She slumped to the floor and put her head in her hands. "If you haven't seen them, I've totally run out of ideas. All I want is to go ice-skating on Mirror Lake!"

Squeak put her paw around her big sister, then jumped up. She began searching in her closet. For a moment, Ruby wondered if she *did* have her skates after all, but then Squeak spun around holding a very dusty old brown box.

She opened the lid. "You can use these ones!" Squeak said.

Ruby stared at her old ice skates. She'd grown out of them last year and they'd been handed down to Squeak.

"Mom says I can't go ice-skating until I've got rid of my cold," Squeak explained. "So you can use them. I don't mind!"

Now Ruby felt even worse for not playing with her sister. Squeak was being so kind to her, even though Ruby hadn't exactly been nice.

"But they're too small," Ruby said.

"Try them," Squeak said, taking one out of the box. "I'm totally sure you'll be able to squeeze your paws in. They're still a bit too big for me."

So Ruby sat down on the rose-petal rug and unlaced one of the skates to try. She pushed her paw inside while Squeak pushed the skate onto her paw.

"Nearly!" Squeak said, but Ruby's paw was

getting so squashed inside the skate, and she only had her toes in so far. They pushed ... and pushed ... and pushed ...

But Ruby's paw just wouldn't fit. Ruby fell backward onto the floor. "It's no good," she said, feeling tears spring to her eyes. "But thank you, Squeak."

"Let's try again!" Squeak said. "Maybe we'll be luckier with the other paw?"

Ruby got up slowly, shaking her head. "Even if the other skate fits, I can't go skating on just one paw. Unless I find my new skates, I'm not going to be able to go skating this winter!"

FIVE

Mirror Lake

Ruby went back to her bedroom, feeling miserable. She lay down on her daisy-petal bedspread and stared at the ceiling, wondering what her friends were doing. Star would be practicing her flips, and the others might be playing ice tag or doing laps around the lake, seeing who could skate the fastest. They always took turns

being the judge, watching on the side to see who won the race.

Ruby sat up suddenly. Even if she didn't have her ice skates, she could still join in. She could judge the races and help Star to perfect her ice-skating moves. At least then she would be back outside with her friends. And maybe one of them would have an idea of where her skates might be.

She took her notebook from her desk just in case she found any clues about where her skates were, then hopped into the kitchen. "I'm going to Mirror Lake," she told her dad, who was stirring something that smelled like tomatoes and onions with a sprinkling of pepper.

"All right," her dad replied without looking

around. That was lucky—Ruby didn't want him to notice she didn't have her skates with her.

Ruby ran as fast as she could to Mirror Lake, which wasn't easy in the thick snow. She hopped high from paw to paw, and was soon out of breath. She passed lots of bunnies carrying their ice skates toward the lake—or on their way home from skating. She looked up at the clock tower as she went by, but there was no sign of the Weather Rabbit. Ruby wondered just how long it would snow for. It could stop at any time!

I have to find my skates before the snow stops! she thought. *But there's lots of time to search before the school trip on Monday. Mr. Nibble wouldn't have planned the trip if he thought the ice would be melted by then.*

Panting, Ruby scampered onto Paradise Beach, snow crunching under her paws as she headed across it to reach Mirror Lake. It was funny to see the usually yellow beach covered in white snow. There were bunnies every-where, busy making all sorts of snow creatures. And now she could *hear* the lake, too, like the most mesmerizing orchestra, with deep notes of cellos and the tinkling of flutes. When the lake iced over and bunnies skated on it, Mirror Lake became even more

magical—it played music! Not only that, but the tunes always seemed to match the rhythm of the skating bunnies.

Ruby's eyes filled with tears. She wasn't sure if it was the beautiful music that made her cry, or the thought of not being able to skate.

"I'll totally find my skates tomorrow," she told herself as the lake full of bunnies came into view. Ruby spotted her friends on one side of the lake and sped up to reach them.

Diamond was already looking over and waving to Ruby. She skated slowly to the edge of the lake to meet her. "It's so much fun," said Diamond in her soft, quiet voice as the music changed to an upbeat brass band,

with lots of tooting trumpets. "Aren't you going to skate?"

"No, I ... um ... ," Ruby began.

"Hi, Ruby," said Twinkle spinning over across the ice toward them. "Where are your skates?"

Ruby looked at her friends, blinked, and burst into tears.

As Diamond put a paw around Ruby, Sky and Star came skating over, too. "What's the matter?" Star asked.

"My skates are gone!" Ruby sobbed. "I've looked for them *everywhere*."

Sky frowned. "Hey, you showed them to me last weekend. They were in the box in the cupboard!"

"I know," said Ruby. "But now they're not

there, and I don't know *where* they are."

"That's such pawful luck!" squeaked Twinkle. "To lose them just when Mirror Lake has iced over."

Ruby nodded and sniffed. "Have any of you seen them?"

"Nope," said Sky. "But hey, we'll help you find them."

"Not now," said Ruby. "I came to watch you. It's heaps better than not enjoying Mirror Lake at all. I'm sure I'll find them soon—and I have the whole weekend before the school trip on Monday."

Star patted Ruby on the shoulder. "Let's look now." She began to step off the ice, but Ruby shook her head.

"No, really—you all enjoy the skating. It'd be awesome if you can help me over the weekend, but you're here now, and it would be a waste not to skate."

Her friends tried to argue, but Ruby kept shaking her head. She held up her notebook. "I'll make a new list of places where the skates might be. And I can judge all your skating races. Want to do one now?"

"If you're sure?" chirruped Sky.

"Positive!" Ruby replied. She sat down on the soft snow while Star drew two lines across the ice—one for the start line and one for the finish.

The lake's music switched to a drumming beat as Sky, Twinkle, Star, and Diamond lined

up at the start. Ruby shouted, "Ready, steady, scamper!"

Star was quickly out ahead, her golden paws sliding powerfully across the ice. Diamond wasn't far behind her, moving smoothly and gracefully, her white fluffy tail

bobbing about. Sky was at the back, but she didn't seem to mind—in fact, she was doing flips and spins as she raced, not seeming to care whether she won or not.

"Star's the winner!" Ruby called out as Star sped past the finish line and almost hurtled into a group of bunnies playing ice tag.

The friends did another race—this time skating backward—and Twinkle was the clear winner. "I've been practicing walking backward!" he said. "You should try it sometime— it's hopping good fun!"

Star started trying out her flips, while Ruby watched and told her if they were smooth or not. Then the four friends began doing laps on the lake, and the music changed

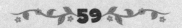

to soft, flowing saxophones. Ruby looked down at her notebook and took out her barkpen.

Places my ice skates might be:
- ~~At home~~
- At school

She crossed out "At home" because she'd already searched everywhere there. Ruby couldn't remember taking her skates to school, but it was the only other place she could think of.

She looked up and gazed across Mirror Lake. Its shiny surface reflected the snow clouds in the sky, pretty little snowflakes

still falling gently from them. Ruby scanned the skating bunnies for anyone wearing a red pair of skates, but not a single bunny was! Anyway, she didn't think any bunny would have stolen them from her. The only creature that might have done that would be Hiss, an annoying ferret who sometimes snuck into the burrow. But Ruby hadn't seen him for a while.

She turned the page of her notebook and began sketching a picture of her ice skates.

"Phew, I'm as tired as a tortoise!" said Twinkle, skating over to the edge of the lake beside Ruby. "What are you doing?" he asked.

Ruby looked up and showed Twinkle the

page of her notebook. "I'm trying to draw my skates, but I can't get the laces right."

Twinkle sat down next to her, shuffling his fluffy green tail into the snow. "Can I help?"

"Oh, yes please, that would be awesome!" said Ruby, passing Twinkle her barkpen.

Soon, the drawing was finished, and Ruby used a ribbon from her tail to tie it up on a nearby tree. She wrote her name and the address of her burrow on it, and smiled. She felt a lot better now, especially with her friends helping.

"We'll spend all weekend searching if we have to!" squeaked Twinkle, linking his arm into Ruby's. "I'm a zillion percent certain we'll find them!"

Ruby smiled at her friend, deciding not to tell him that there was no such thing as a zillion percent.

"Thanks, Twinkle," Ruby replied. "I'm so lucky to have such amazing friends."

SIX

Saturday at School

"Aren't you going out ice-skating?" Ruby's mom asked the next morning, popping her head into Ruby's bedroom.

"Not right now." Ruby looked around. "I'm tidying my room." *That wasn't really even a fib,* she thought.

Ruby's mom made a face as she gazed at

Ruby's floor. "Good idea," she said. "You usually don't let it get this messy."

Her mom pulled the door closed again and Ruby carried on with what she was doing—carefully searching her room in case she'd missed her ice skates the first time. She'd woken up extra early to do it before meeting her friends, and she secretly hoped she'd find them so they could just go straight to Mirror Lake.

But she heard a knock and realized she'd run out of time. Deep down she knew the skates weren't in her room anyway. She'd hunted for them in here twice now!

Ruby ran to the door, where Star, Diamond, Sky, and Twinkle stood, all wrapped up in

woolly hats and scarves. "We're here to help you find your skates!" squeaked Twinkle.

"Shh!" whispered Ruby. "I don't want my parents to know!"

Ruby's dad appeared beside her. "Aren't you going skating today?" he said, noticing that none of them were carrying their ice skates.

"Not yet, Dad," Ruby replied, thinking quickly. "We...um...we're waiting until Petal can come, too. She's at home helping out while her mom is getting better."

Ruby's dad nodded, and his curly whiskers bounced around. "Oh yes, I hope she's better soon. I took her a box of elder bark yesterday to help with her sprain."

"Right, Dad," said Ruby, pulling on her ear-muffs and not really listening. She wanted to leave before he asked too many questions. "Bye!"

She rushed out of the burrow, tugging her friends after her. As they walked along, Ruby showed her friends her list of places the skates might be. "I've looked everywhere at

home," she said. "So maybe they're at school!"

"I don't remember you bringing your ice skates to school," said Star, looking doubtful.

"I don't either." Ruby frowned. "But I can't think of where else they could be. Will you help me look?"

"Of course we will!" said Twinkle.

Sky nodded. "We'll find your skates by Monday, sure thing!"

Diamond took Ruby's paw and gave it a squeeze. "We're not going skating until you can come, too."

The five friends scampered toward Dandelion School, their paws making light prints in the snow. *It was strange heading*

there on a Saturday, Star thought. Normally they'd be surrounded by lots of bunnies going in the same direction, but today they were the only ones walking through the gates. They crossed the dandelion field toward the large oak tree, where their class-room was.

Twinkle darted into the classroom first, expecting it to be empty, and squealed when something moved in the corner.

"It's okay," said Diamond, who had the best eyesight out of her friends. "It's just Mr. Nibble."

Their teacher looked up from his desk, and peered over at them. "Oh, hello, Twinkle, Diamond, Ruby, Star, and Sky," he said, while

chewing on a dandelion stalk. "Have you forgotten it's Saturday?"

"No, Mr. Nibble," Star replied. "We're just here looking for something."

Mr. Nibble walked over, a bundle of barknotes under his arm. "What is it? Perhaps I've seen it."

Ruby wondered whether or not to tell Mr. Nibble, but decided it couldn't hurt. Maybe he *had* seen them.

"It's my new ice skates," said Ruby. "I've lost them. They're red and shiny and just really, really awesome . . ."

Mr. Nibble chewed harder on the stalk and his eyes crinkled as he thought.

Ruby's heart fluttered in her chest. *Maybe*

he knows where they are and we can go skating right away! she thought.

He took the dandelion stalk from his mouth and shook his head. "Sorry, Ruby. I haven't seen any ice skates. Lost school ties? Yes—I have a

hundred of them. Barkpens, too. But no ice skates. Are you sure they're not at home?"

Ruby nodded. Twinkle turned to her and saw her eyes were red. She looked like she was about to cry.

"But can we look around the classroom anyway?" Twinkle asked.

"Yes, maybe they're in one of the drawers or cupboards!" said Sky.

Mr. Nibble smiled at the bunnies. "You are kind to help your friend like this. Yes, you can look. But if you move things, make sure you put everything back where you found it, okay?"

"Yes!" the friends said together.

Mr. Nibble scampered past them. "Right, I

must get home—I only came here to pick up some tests to grade that I forgot yesterday. I'll see you on Monday. Remember, you should go straight to Mirror Lake for our trip—don't come to school. Ruby, I hope you find your skates before then!"

SEVEN
Sharing Is Caring

"Let's get to work!" said Star, looking around the classroom. "I'll search the cupboards. Diamond, you look through the drawers—they're so dark at the back but you'll be able to see, no problem. Sky, try looking under all the desks—you can lift them up if necessary. And Twinkle, can you look in all the

small places the rest of us can't get to?"

"I'll go around sniffing everywhere," said Ruby. "I'm sure I'll recognize their new shoe smell if they're in here."

The friends began their search. The cupboards and drawers were so full of school things that Star and Diamond had to empty them out to look inside properly. The floor of the classroom got fuller and fuller with crafts, sports equipment, science materials, and folders of work.

"Hey, I've found something!" yelped Sky, holding up Mr. Nibble's desk with one paw.

Ruby rushed over to look. "It's something red!" she said, crouching down so she could slide under the desk. Her heart pounded as she

reached out for the box...but it wasn't the right shape for her skates. Sure enough, when she pulled it out and opened it, it was full of cherry pop sweets.

"Whose are those?" asked Twinkle, licking his lips and wondering if he could take one.

Star peered inside the box. "Mr. Nibble's secret stash perhaps? Anyway, it doesn't matter—let's keep looking!"

With Sky still holding the desk up high, Ruby pushed the box back under, and the friends continued their search.

But by lunchtime, they still hadn't gotten any closer to finding the skates. And they'd been through their whole classroom. It looked worse

than Ruby's room had yesterday, with piles of things all over the floor.

"Let's have some lunch and then search the other classrooms," said Star.

"No, you should all go and skate," Ruby told them. "I can finish looking on my own. You've already done so much this morning."

"No way!" Sky put her hands on her hips. "We're not leaving you now. We're not giving up."

Twinkle held up a basket. "I found a whole basket of carrots when I was searching the food tech drawers. Burrow-tastic, right? They were so far at the back, Mr. Nibble must have forgotten them. We can replace them on Tuesday morning!"

Diamond cleared a space on the floor so they could sit and munch on the carrots, and the friends ate them hungrily. "I'm starving," said Ruby. "All this searching has made me hungry!" *But I would be happy not to eat all day if it meant I found my skates*, she thought.

After they'd eaten lunch, they began looking in the other classrooms—Willow Class, Chestnut Class, Maple Class, and Pine Class. They searched them from top to bottom, just as they'd done in Oak Class, but the closest they'd come was finding a red top hat in Maple Class, which Twinkle guessed belonged to the teacher, Ms. Longwhisker. They'd been taught by her last year, and she

always came to school in the most furbulous hats, Twinkle thought. Once she'd even worn a space helmet!

By the end of the day, when their bellies were rumbling again, hungry for dinner, they had to agree that Ruby's ice skates were definitely nowhere in Dandelion School. Diamond gazed around Pine Class, the last place they'd looked. "We can't leave the classrooms like this. We'll get into huge trouble."

Diamond was right, especially when Mr. Nibble had told them to put everything back afterward.

"I'll come back tomorrow to tidy up all the classrooms," Ruby told her friends, but of course they wouldn't let her do that.

"We'll all do it," said Star.

They spent the whole of Sunday morning cleaning the school. "Thank you," Ruby told her friends as she put the last things back in a drawer. "It would have totally taken ages if I'd done it alone."

"What now?" squeaked Twinkle.

"You have to go skating!" said Ruby. "There's nowhere else to search, and I feel so awful you've spent all your time helping me."

Diamond raised a white paw. "I have an idea," she said softly.

Her friends turned to Diamond, listening carefully.

"We can *all* go skating," Diamond went on.

"We can take turns and share our skates with you, Ruby. Then you get to skate, too!"

Ruby beamed. She wasn't surprised that Diamond had come up with a brilliant idea. Diamond didn't speak a lot, but when she did, she often said something super helpful or clever.

"Sharing is caring!" Sky laughed, doing a little backflip.

"That's a truly great idea." Star was beaming, too. "So let's get back to our burrows to pick up our skates and then run to Mirror Lake!"

Just a few minutes later, the friends had arrived on Paradise Beach. It was still snowing, and Twinkle wondered just how far the sand was buried underneath the thick drifts of snow. Playful piano music was floating over the lake as bunnies skipped and jumped across it.

"You can use mine first," said Twinkle, passing his shiny silver skates to Ruby. "I don't mind watching. In fact, I'm going to build the snowiest, superest snow bunny ever!"

But Ruby looked at the skates doubtfully. They didn't look any bigger than her old ones that were now Squeak's. She sat down on the snow and loosened all the laces before pushing one paw in. It just about fit inside, but she couldn't tie the skate up!

"Um . . . thanks, Twinkle," Ruby said as Twinkle started flinging snow everywhere with his little green paws. "But I don't think I can use your skates. They're awesome—but they're just too small."

"Have mine," said Diamond. "They look more like your size."

Ruby smiled gratefully and tried a paw in Diamond's bright blue skate. It fit much better, and Ruby could pull them up easily. Once she'd put both on, she stepped onto the ice, but the skates were wobbly, her paws too loose inside. Ruby pushed one paw forward carefully, then the other . . .

And fell over, right on her tail.

"Ouch!" Ruby cried as her friends skated over to make sure she was okay. "Don't worry, I'm totally fine! But I don't think I can use your skates, Diamond. They're a bit too big. Thank you, though."

Star looked down at her own skates and

made a face. If Diamond's were too large, then hers definitely would be.

"Mine are smaller," chirruped Sky. She pulled them off quickly and held them out to Ruby.

Ruby smiled as she put them on. "They do feel much better," she said. But when she stood up on the ice, her toes were suddenly all pinched. Ruby started to skate around and tried to ignore the pain, her friends clapping as she finally got her turn on Mirror Lake. She tried a single spin, in time with the whizzing piano notes . . . but it hurt her toes so much that she cried out in pain.

"Did you hurt yourself?" asked Diamond, gliding over.

Ruby shook her head. "No, but Sky's skates are really pinching my toes. It's no good—we

won't be able to take turns after all." Ruby tried to keep smiling, but she could feel her eyes watering and her whiskers drooping. She sat down and took the skates off as her friends crowded around. The lake's music suddenly slowed, in sad violin notes, as if to match Ruby's mood.

"I'm so sorry you couldn't skate after all," Star said.

"It sure stinks," added Sky.

"Such bad luck," Twinkle squeaked. "I was pawsitive some of our skates would fit you!"

Ruby looked up at her friends' kind, concerned faces. "I'm okay," she said. "And I'm so grateful for all you've done to help. But it looks as if I won't get to skate on the school trip after all."

EIGHT
The School Trip

The first thing Ruby did when she woke up on Monday morning was to rush to check if it was still snowing. And then she remembered it didn't really matter because she still hadn't found her skates. It was the day of the school trip. Rather than joining in, she'd just have to watch her friends skating.

Ruby closed the door to her burrow sadly and slumped down at the breakfast table.

"Hop tarts or forest oats?" her dad asked.

Ruby looked up but didn't answer. She wasn't feeling hungry at all. Her tummy was like a rock inside her when she thought about her lost skates. *I'll totally have to tell Mom and Dad now*, she thought. She couldn't keep on fibbing to them, and they'd find out sooner or later.

"Ruby?" Her dad turned from the counter and bent down toward Ruby. "Are you okay?"

She sighed and shook her head. "I—"

A knock at the door cut Ruby off. Her mom opened it. "Oh, hello, Petal. Is your mom feeling better?"

Petal smiled. "Yes, much, much better,

thank you. I've come to return the elder bark. Mom didn't need to use it after all." She held out a box in her paws and Ruby did a double take.

The next moment she leaped up from the breakfast table and ran over to her friend. "Are you totally sure that's elder bark?" she asked. "Can I take a look?"

Petal passed the red box to Ruby, frowning with confusion. "That's what your dad said. But we never had to open it."

Ruby lifted the lid slowly, not daring to get her hopes up. She sniffed and breathed in the new shoe smell she'd been searching for the last few days. *Maybe that's just how elder bark smells*, she told herself.

She took another breath and whipped off the lid—and her heart nearly leaped out of her chest. "My ice skates!" she yelped, jumping up and down while holding the shiny red skates aloft.

"Huh?" said Petal. "What's going on?"

Ruby turned to her parents and put the

skates on the table. "Dad, did you check in the box before you gave it to Petal's mom?"

"No," he said. "Your mom just told me to get the box from the cupboard. It was the only one I could see!"

Ruby's mom shook her head, making her curly whiskers bounce. "The elder bark box is much smaller than that one, and it's white, not red!"

"Dad!" Ruby said. "Those were my ice skates. I've been looking for them everywhere!"

Her dad's eyes grew wide. "I'm so sorry, Ruby! But why didn't you tell us you couldn't find them?"

Ruby looked down at the poppy-flower rug on the floor. "I knew they cost you a lot and I

didn't want you to know I had lost them until I was totally sure of it!"

Her mom hopped over and patted Ruby on the back. "Oh, Ruby, I wondered why you'd been acting so strangely this week!"

Ruby couldn't be annoyed at her dad for long—after all, the most important thing

was that her skates were found. She would finally be able to skate on Mirror Lake! She threw her paws around Petal and danced about. Petal joined in, although she still had absolutely no idea what was going on.

"My skates!" Ruby started to explain once she'd finally stopped dancing. "I couldn't find them anywhere, and really thought they were lost."

"Your dad gave them to my mom by mistake?" Petal said, realizing what had happened.

"Exactly!" said Ruby.

Squeak ran out from her bedroom. "Your skates, Ruby! I told you I hadn't taken them!"

"I'm sorry for thinking that, Squeak," said

Ruby. "Actually, Dad gave them away, but he didn't know. All that matters now is that I have them!" She turned to Petal. "Are you ready for the school trip?"

"Absolutely!" said Petal, holding up her backpack, which contained her own ice skates.

"Awesome. Then let's go!"

Ruby's dad held out two hop tarts to Ruby and Petal, and they munched them on the way to Mirror Lake. It took Ruby the whole journey there to explain just what had happened that weekend while Petal had been helping out at home.

"It was lucky you brought back the elder bark this morning," Ruby finished. "Otherwise, my

skates would still be lost, and I wouldn't be able to join in today."

"So very lucky!" Petal agreed.

They reached Mirror Lake and Ruby gasped. It was silent and totally empty of bunnies!

"It's still so early," Petal said. "Quick, let's get on the ice before anyone else arrives. I've never been ice-skating with no one else here!"

"Me neither!" Ruby slid one paw into a skate, and it fit perfectly. It wasn't loose or a bit too tight—just perfect.

Moments later, Ruby and Petal stepped onto the ice, and delicate harp music began to play. It was as if their paws were making the music! They skated along, hand in hand. Ruby couldn't help beaming from ear to ear. The skates felt

as comfortable as slippers, and she zoomed around the lake so fast that Petal had to let go. "Sorry, Petal!" Ruby said, turning to stop, but Petal waved her on.

"No need to apologize! You've been waiting for this for a long time. But I just like to go slower—I'm less likely to fall over that way."

Ruby grinned and sped up again, pushing one paw forward and then the other. The wind rippled past her ears and she batted her eyelids in the falling snow.

"Hey, Ruby, Petal!" came a shout from Paradise Beach. Ruby did a double spin on one skate to turn around and saw the rest of her best friends arriving at the lake.

When they saw Ruby was wearing her

beautiful ice skates, they ran onto the ice to hug her.

"You found them!" Twinkle squeaked. "What in burrow happened!"

Ruby explained the story as she and her friends skated around the lake holding paws.

"I should have looked in the box. I'm sorry!" Petal said when Ruby had finished.

But Ruby shook her head. "You couldn't have known. And it doesn't matter now—I have them, and it feels AMAZING. Ice-skating is even more awesome than I remember!"

Soon the rest of Oak Class had arrived and were on the ice, waiting for Mr. Nibble and Poppy Lightpaw to arrive.

"There she is," whispered Diamond as

she spotted a tall yellow rabbit with short pointy ears over on the opposite side of Paradise Beach.

Ruby took a deep breath in awe and watched Mr. Nibble guide Poppy over the beach toward their class.

"Hello, Oak Class," Mr. Nibble said. For once he wasn't eating anything. *Maybe he wants to impress Poppy!* thought Star.

"This is the talented Poppy Lightpaw," Mr. Nibble continued, waving her forward onto the ice.

The lake's music changed to bright, bouncy clarinets as Poppy did a hop and skip onto the ice. She glided so smoothly she looked like she was flying.

"I'm so delighted to be here!" Poppy said in a
rich, happy voice. "Who wants to learn some
top ice-skating tricks?"

The entire class put up their hands at once
and Poppy grinned. "All right, then let's get
started!"

They spent the whole morning on Mirror

Lake, learning skips and spins and even double flips. Ruby didn't stop smiling, especially when Poppy pointed at her skates and said, "Oh, how lovely your skates are! You must take good care of those!"

Ruby nodded. "I will!" *I'm going to label the box VERY CLEARLY as soon as I get home,* Ruby thought. *Or maybe, as they're so beautiful, I'll never take them off!*

You're in luck!

Read on for a peek
at where the hoppiest, floppiest,
pluckiest, luckiest bunnies around
started their adventures!

ONE
At the Tail Salon

It was a sunny Sunday afternoon in Bright
Burrow, and Ruby, Sky, Star, Petal, and
Diamond scampered along the shiny green
cobbles of Cucumber Row. The five friends
were heading toward their favorite tail salon,
Fur Real, where they went every Sunday to
have their tails trimmed, brushed, and styled.

"Ooh, look!" said Sky, skipping up to a gift shop called Mrs. Whiskers's Pawfect Presents. "Bunny balloons!" She pressed her extremely furry head to the window. It was filled with brightly colored balloons that had been shaped, stretched, and tied into floating rabbit figures.

Everyone turned to look at the impressive balloon display, apart from Star who kept striding ahead. "We'll be lucky to get spots at Fur Real if we don't hurry up," she said.

Sky took a last longing look at the balloons, then ran to catch up with her friends.

"I'm sure we can go there later," said Petal when she saw Sky's disappointed face and turned-down whiskers.

They reached the entrance of Fur Real, where glittering disco balls spun across the top of the window. Star pushed open the door, making the bells on it tinkle like a triangle. As she was about to step in, a tiny blur of mint-green fur hurtled past them outside.

"Twinkle?" Ruby called out into the street.

Their friend Twinkle was supposed to meet them earlier that day, but he'd never shown up.

The little mint-green blur skidded to a stop, grinned, and did a double backflip over to his friends.

"It's lucky we bumped into you!" said Petal. "Is everything all right?" she asked Twinkle as the friends hopped into Fur Real. The walls were covered in glossy pictures of tails of every size, shape, and color.

"Yes, I'm fine, thanks," Twinkle squeaked. "Furbulous, in fact! Look, that's lucky, too— there are six spare seats for us!"

They took turns dipping their tails in the bathtub full of Bunny Bubbles in the corner of the salon, then jumped up onto the line of toadstool chairs. Beside each chair stood a smiling salon worker with a comb in one paw and a pair of scissors in the other.

"So where have you been?" asked Ruby as she shook out her wet tail.

"At home, doing a bit of paw-painting," said Twinkle. One of the tail-dressers handed him a Five-Flower Fizz drink, and he took a long, slurping sip through the straw. "I think it might be my very best one yet! Why do you ask?"

"You're late!" said Star, with a twitch of her nose. "We were supposed to meet this morning."

Twinkle flicked his tiny ears up in surprise. "Is it the afternoon already?" he squeaked. "Oh, sorry! I lost track of time. What burrow-tastic adventures did I miss?"

Ruby held up a red paw and counted her four fingers. "So much! We went for brunch at Crocus Cafe, rode the Clover Train to Paradise Beach, went swimming in Mirror Lake, then had a totally delicious picnic! Diamond even found a magical shell in the sand on Paradise Beach, didn't you, Diamond?"

Diamond leaned over to Twinkle and held out a glowing yellow shell. "It lights up like magic," she said in her shy, quiet voice. "I was so lucky to find it! I'm going to put it on my bedside table at home."

The bunnies often went digging at Paradise Beach, not just because they *loved* to dig, but because sometimes they could find magical surprises hidden in the sand.

"What do you call a rabbit who's late?" asked Sky all of a sudden in her chirpy voice.

The friends went quiet while they tried to think of the answer to Sky's joke.

"Oh, I know, I know!" said Star with a nod. "Paw timing!"

"Nope," said Sky, shaking her fluffy blue head. "Bunny-hind!" Sky thumped her foot as she laughed at her own joke. "Get it? Behind . . . bunny-hind!"

Her friends giggled—everyone except Star. "I think paw timing was better . . . ," said Star. "You know—*poor* timing?"

"Anyway," Petal said quickly, thinking she'd better change the subject before her friends started arguing. "What is everyone having done today? I've been wondering whether I should get my tail dyed red . . ."

Twinkle turned to Petal and frowned. "Won't it clash with your pink fur? And your tail is a furbulous color already, Petal. So pearly-pink! Whereas Star . . . Star, you could really pull off a red tail. With your yellow body, you'd look like a beautiful bundle of fire!"

"I don't think so!" said Star. "I'm having just a trim and blow-dry, like usual. I want my tail to look perfect for Bounce-a-Lot on Saturday."

Bounce-a-Lot was a festival that took place in Bright Burrow every year, featuring all sorts of bouncing events. Every Lucky Bunny looked forward to it, whether they were chosen as Bouncers to take part in the festival, or

came along to watch the amazing bouncing displays.

"I'd forgotten about Bounce-a-Lot," said Petal, flapping her big ears in excitement. "I don't think I'll be lucky enough to get chosen as a Bouncer, but I don't mind at all. I just love to watch!"

Diamond jumped down from the toadstool

chair to check out her tail in the mirror. The tail-dresser had fluffed and combed it into a perfect heart shape.

"That looks absolutely stunning," squeaked Twinkle, putting his paws to his face in admiration. "You're so lucky to have fur like that. I wish mine was thick enough for that style!"

Diamond smiled shyly. "Thanks," she said quietly as she hopped to the door. "See you tomorrow for school?"

"Aren't you coming to Strawberry Fields later?" Ruby asked Diamond. "They're showing the movie 101 *Velveteen Rabbits*. It's supposed to be awesome!" Strawberry Fields was Bright Burrow's theater and cinema. Alongside Paradise Beach, it was one of the friends' favorite places, partly because it served the most delicious strawberry shakes—which refilled like magic whenever a bunny reached the bottom of the cup.

Diamond gave a little shake of her shimmering white head. "No, I can't come tonight. I've got science homework to do. I'll see you in the morning." The bells at the door tinkled as she opened it. She scampered out toward Warren Street, the maze of burrows where all the Lucky Bunnies lived.

"Hey, what do you call a squished strawberry?" chirped Sky. Her blue eyes twinkled with the thought of her new joke. This time she answered before anyone could guess. "Jam!"

Everyone laughed, the tail-dressers, too.

"That was much better, Sky," said Star. "It was actually quite funny."

"Tell us another one?" Petal asked. She sat forward on her toadstool chair to listen, and her long, drooping ears almost touched the floor.

"Sorry, nope, I can't right now," Sky said. The tail-dresser gave Sky's very furry fur a final brush, and Sky leaped from her chair. She did a dizzying jump and spin in front of the mirror, which undid almost all the tail-dresser's hard work, although Sky didn't seem to notice. "Star has reminded me—I've got to go home and practice my bounce-moves for Bounce-a-Lot," Sky explained. "Mom said she'd buy some hopcorn, too, to help give me extra springing power. Ooh, I can't wait for next Saturday!"

The bells tinkled again as Sky rushed out into Cucumber Row with a hop and a wave.

"Who do you think Mr. Nibble will choose to be Bouncers?" said Twinkle as his tail-dresser snipped oh-so-carefully at his tiny little tail. Tomorrow, their teacher at Dandelion School would decide who from their class would be taking part in the Bounce-a-Lot festival.

"Maybe Mr. Nibble will choose everyone?" said Petal hopefully. She couldn't bear to see any of her friends disappointed.

"I don't think so!" Star replied. "Only six from each class are chosen. And having everyone wouldn't be fair when *some* bunnies have been preparing for it all year." Star herself was one of those bunnies. She always practiced hard, and it paid off—she'd been chosen as a Bouncer every single year so far.

"Life's not always fair," said Ruby with a flick of her curly red whiskers. "It's important to work hard, but sometimes you also need luck!"